ALAN DURANT

Illustrated by
ANNABEL HUDSON

MA   )KS

For Paula, who lit a candle – A.D.
For Simon. ✗ ✗ ✗ – A.H.

First published by Kingfisher 2003

This edition published 2012 by Macmillan Children's Books
a division of Macmillan Publishers Limited
20 New Wharf Road, London N1 9RR
Basingstoke and Oxford
Associated companies throughout the world
www.panmacmillan.com

ISBN 978-1-4472-2218-7

A CIP catalogue record for this book is available from the British Library.

Printed in China

Contents

Brown Bear in the Dark

Brown Bear woke with a start.

Crash! Thump!

Something hit the ground so hard
that Brown Bear's house hopped
and wobbled.

Brown Bear sat up in bed.

"Oh!" he cried.

He looked at his clock.

The time was eight o'clock.

It should be light by now,

thought Brown Bear. But it wasn't.

Brown Bear switched on his
bedside light.
He got out of bed and padded
to the window.
He pulled back the curtains,
but all he could see was dark.
His clock said it was morning,
but his window said it was night.

Brown Bear
sat on his bed
and thought.
He thought
about the crash
in the wood.
He thought
about the dark.
He thought
about the time.

Suddenly, he *knew* what had happened.
The sun had fallen out of the sky!
"Oh dear, oh dear!" Brown Bear
said to himself.

He thought about
the wood outside
without the sun
in the sky.
It would be dark
and cold – *very* dark and *very* cold.

Brown Bear shivered.

There might be nasty things out there.

There might be horrible witches

with green faces or slimy, slithery

creatures with sharp teeth

or bear-eating monsters . . .

Tramp, tramp, tramp!

Someone was climbing up the stairs.

The monsters were coming to get him!

Brown Bear dived under the bed.

"Go away!" he moaned.

"I don't want to be eaten."

"Brown Bear, it's only me,"

called Bunny.

Bunny lived downstairs.

She was Brown Bear's best friend.

"Did you hear that terrible crash?

Whatever could it be?" said Bunny.

Brown Bear crawled out from

under his bed.

"I know what it was," he said. "Bunny,

the sun has fallen out of the sky!"

He took Bunny to the window and
showed her the dark outside.
"This is awful," said Bunny.
"We should tell Chimp."
Chimp was their friend.
He lived just across the wood.

"Yes," agreed Brown Bear.

He thought for a moment.

"But we'll have to go outside,"

he said unhappily.

"Of course," said Bunny.

"But it's cold and dark and there might

be nasty things out there,"

said Brown Bear. "There might be

witches or slimy, slithery creatures

or even bear-eating monsters."

Bunny went pale.

There might be

bunny-eating

monsters out there too,

she thought.

Knock, knock!

Bunny and Brown Bear leapt
and screamed.

Brown Bear dived
under the bed again and
Bunny hid behind the curtains.

Knock, knock!

There was a monster at the front door!

"There's no one here!"

wailed Brown Bear.

"G-g-g-go a-w-w-way,"

stammered Bunny.

"Brown Bear, open the door!"

called a familiar voice. "It's Chimp!"

Brown Bear got out from under
the bed and crossed the room.
With trembling paws,
he opened the front door.
"Quick, Chimp! I've got
something important to
tell you," Brown Bear gabbled.
He grabbed Chimp and pulled him
inside, slamming the door behind him.
"What is it, Brown Bear?" asked Chimp.
"What's the matter?"
"It's the sun, Chimp," cried Brown Bear.
"It's fallen out of the sky!"
"And the wood is dark and full of
horrible monsters," added Bunny.

Chimp frowned. "I didn't see any
horrible monsters," he said.
"And the wood isn't dark. It's bright.
The sun is shining. Come and see."
Chimp went to the front door and
opened it wide. Sunlight spilled in.

Brown Bear blinked and rubbed his eyes.

"Oh," he said.

"Oh," said Bunny.

Brown Bear looked at the window
and pointed.

"But the window's dark," he said.

Chimp led Brown Bear and
Bunny outside. "Look," he said.
A big tree had fallen outside Brown
Bear's window. "That's why it was
so dark in your room."

Brown Bear and Bunny
stood in the bright sunlight,
staring at the big tree
and feeling a little silly.

"Well," said Chimp, "I think we should move this tree, don't you?"

"Good idea," Bunny agreed.

"Mmm," said Brown Bear. "But first I think we should go inside and have some breakfast. All this excitement has made me hungry!"

"Now, that," said Chimp with a smile, "is a *very* good idea!"

Brown Bear Gets in Shape

One morning, Brown Bear looked

down and got a nasty surprise.

He could not see his feet.

All that he could see was his big,

round tummy.

The more he looked, the bigger and
rounder his tummy seemed to be.
"Oh," said Brown Bear. "Oh dear.
How tubby I have grown."
He went downstairs to see Bunny.

"Hello, Bunny," said Brown Bear.

"Hello, Brown Bear," said Bunny.

Brown Bear looked at Bunny.

Bunny's tummy wasn't tubby.

She could easily see her feet.

"Bunny," said Brown Bear,

"I want to be the same shape as you.

What should I do?"

Bunny thought for a moment.

"What do you eat?" she asked at last.

"Honey," said Brown Bear. "What

do *you* eat?"

"I eat lettuce and carrots," said Bunny.

"Why don't you try eating lettuce and

carrots too?"

So Brown Bear tried lettuce and carrots

. . . for *one whole day.*

He had carrot juice

and lettuce leaves

for breakfast.

He had lettuce
sandwiches and
carrot cake
for lunch.

He had lettuce soup
and carrot sticks
for dinner.

But he didn't like it very much and he
still couldn't see his feet.

When he looked down, his tummy
looked bigger than ever.
"Oh dear, this is no good," he said.
"Perhaps Chimp will be able to help."
So Brown Bear went to visit Chimp.
Chimp's tummy wasn't tubby.
He could see his feet.

"Chimp," said Brown Bear,
"I wish my tummy was the same
shape as yours. What do you eat?"
"I eat bananas," said Chimp.
"OK," said Brown Bear. "Then I
shall eat bananas too."

Brown Bear ate
bananas for
one whole week.
He ate banana bread

and drank banana

milkshakes.

He even ate
banana skins!

He liked bananas a lot more than lettuce or carrots, but his tummy was still the same shape and he still couldn't see his feet.

"This is no good," he sighed.

Bunny had another idea.
"Why don't you come for a hop
with me?" she said. "Exercise
is good for getting in shape."
"OK," said Brown Bear.
So Brown Bear and Bunny
went for a hop through the forest.

Hop,

Hop,

Hop!

"This is fun!" said Brown Bear.

But then . . .

squelch, squerch, squish!

Brown Bear hopped so hard he was
in mud up to his middle!

"Help! Help!" cried Brown Bear.
Chimp heard the noise and came out
of his house to help.

Chimp and Bunny pulled Brown Bear
out of the mud.

Then they took him to Chimp's house
and helped him get clean again.
"Why don't we all go to the gym,"
said Chimp.
"That's where I go
to get in shape."

Brown Bear loved the gym.

He leapt on this

and he pulled on that.

He did sit-ups

and star jumps.

Chimp threw him a rope. "Hey,

Brown Bear, climb up this!" he called.

Brown Bear climbed up the rope.

Then he swung onto another and
another and another.

"This is fun!" cried Brown Bear.

But then *crack! crunch! crash!*
Brown Bear bashed
into the wall,
fell off the rope

and bumped on his bottom.
"Ow!" howled Brown Bear.

"It's no good," said Brown Bear,
looking down at his tummy.
"My tummy is still round and tubby.
I'll never be able to change my shape."

Bunny looked at Brown Bear.
"Brown Bear," she said, "I like
your shape. It's, well, bear-shaped."
"Yes," agreed Chimp. "Bears are
supposed to have round tummies.
Have you ever seen a bear with a
flat tummy?"

Brown Bear thought.

He thought very hard.

"Well, no," he said at last.

"I don't think I have."

"You have your shape

and we have ours,"

said Bunny.

Brown Bear looked

down at his big, round,

bear-shaped tummy.

"Mmm, perhaps you're right," he said.

Then he smiled.

"I love my tummy," sighed Brown Bear

happily and he gave it a little pat.

Then he frowned.

"You don't think it's looking a little flat, do you?" he asked anxiously. "NO!" said Bunny and Chimp together. But Brown Bear went to get some honey . . . just in case.

About the Author and Illustrator

Alan Durant has written many stories for children of all ages. Most of his books have started life as tales told to his own children. "Brown Bear, Chimp and Bunny are based on three of my daughter Josie's beanie babies," he says. "She asked me to make up a story about them one evening – and that's how 'Brown Bear Gets in Shape' came about."

Annabel Hudson worked as a lawyer before becoming a full-time illustrator. "Being able to draw and paint all day is brilliant fun," she says. She also enjoys making collages, ripping up bits of paper and sticking them together. Like Brown Bear, Annabel loves honey, "especially toast or crumpets with lots of butter and lots of honey on top."

Here are some more **I Am Reading** books for you to enjoy:

ALBERT'S RACCOON

ALLIGATOR TAILS AND CROCODILE CAKES

BARN PARTY

CAPTAIN PEPPER'S PETS

DOUGHNUT DANGER

THE GIANT POSTMAN

GRANDAD'S DINOSAUR

JJ RABBIT AND THE MONSTER

JOE LION'S BIG BOOTS

JUST MABEL

KIT'S CASTLE

MISS WIRE AND THE THREE KIND MICE

MR COOL

MRS HIPPO'S PIZZA PARLOUR

NOISY NEIGHBOURS

PRINCESS ROSA'S WINTER

RICKY'S RAT GANG

SMALL BAD WOLF

WATCH OUT, WILLIAM